ROBERT LOUIS STEVENSON

• • •

BLOCK CITY

• • •

illustrated by

ASHLEY WOLFF

A Puffin Unicorn

"Block City" is a poem by Robert Louis Stevenson.

Illustrations copyright © 1988 by Ashley Wolff

All rights reserved.

Unicorn is a registered trademark of Dutton Children's Books.

Library of Congress number 87-33397
ISBN 0-14-054551-4

Published in the United States by Dutton Children's Books,
a division of Penguin Books USA Inc.
375 Hudson Street, New York, New York 10014

Designer: Barbara Powderly

Printed in Hong Kong by South China Printing Co.
First Unicorn Edition 1992
10 9 8 7 6 5 4 3

PUFFIN BOOKS

Published by the Penguin Group
Penguin Books USA Inc.,
375 Hudson Street, New York, New York 10014, U.S.A.
Penguin Books Ltd,
27 Wrights Lane, London W8 5TZ, England
Penguin Books Australia Ltd,
Ringwood, Victoria, Australia
Penguin Books Canada Ltd,
10 Alcorn Avenue, Toronto, Ontario, Canada M4V 3B2
Penguin Books (N.Z.) Ltd,
182-190 Wairau Road, Auckland 10, New Zealand

Penguin Books Ltd,
Registered Offices: Harmondsworth, Middlesex, England

for my dear Brennan

What are you able to
build with your blocks?
Castles and palaces,
temples and docks.

Rain may keep raining,
and others go roam,

But I can be happy and building at home.

Let the sofa be mountains, the carpet be sea,

There I'll establish a city for me:

A kirk
and a mill
and a palace beside,

And a harbor as well where
my vessels may ride.

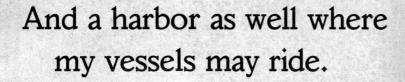

Great is the palace
with pillar and wall,

A sort of a tower on the top of it all,
And steps coming down in an orderly way
To where my toy vessels lie safe in the bay.

This one is sailing
 and that one is moored:
Hark to the song
 of the sailors on board!

And see on the steps
of my palace, the kings

Coming and going
with presents and things!

Now I have done with it,
down let it go!

All in a moment
the town is laid low.

Block upon block lying scattered and free,
What is there left of my town by the sea?

Yet as I saw it, I see it again,
The kirk and the palace,
   the ships and the men,
And as long as I live,
   and where'er I may be,
I'll always remember my town
   by the sea.